Ooboo and friends
The Magical Rocketship

Written by AMY J. BENICKI
Designed by ANTHONY M. BENICKI

About the Author

Amy J. Benicki is an elementary school teacher, wife, and mother of two in Surprise, Arizona. As a child, she always dreamed of writing stories that would be passed on from one generation to the next. She put those dreams on hold as she raised her own children and began a career in education. Throughout her teaching career, she saw the excitement in her students' faces as they read stories, therefore inspiring her to begin her career writing children's books.

Ooboo and friends ™
The Magical Rocketship

Written by AMY J. BENICKI

Designed by ANTHONY M. BENICKI

www.Oobooandfriends.com

ISBN-10: 1523682175
ISBN-13: 978-1523682171

To my loving husband

Tony, you have always inspired me to follow my dreams.You encouraged me to go into teaching, and for that I am thankful. You encouraged me to write, and for that I am grateful. You are a very caring husband and father, and I appreciate you very much. You are my soulmate and I love you more than words can say.

To my wonderful son and daughter

Anthony and Ashley, I am the proudest mother in the world. You make me so happy. You make my day, my week, my month, my year, my life. I thank God for both of you every day. As young adults, you have many adventures awaiting you. Enjoy life and always follow your dreams.

Hi. My name is Ooboo and I love spending time outside. I am the luckiest kangaroo ever! Why you ask? Well, because I live in a treehouse, of course! I also get to travel the world with my friends RoRo, Camille, Jack, and Tippy! But, it wasn't always this way...

Our very first adventure began during my birthday party. Let me tell you all about it!

It was a Saturday afternoon. My friends RoRo, Camille, Jack, and Tippy arrived on time, with gifts.

I *love* gifts, so I quickly took them out of their hands and raced into the house.

RoRo handed me his gift. "It's out of this world!" he said. I opened it slowly, and inside the package was a miniature rocketship.

"What am I supposed to do with this?" I asked.

"It's a magical rocketship, and if we close our eyes and count to five, we will instantly be in space," he replied.

"That's silly," Jack said. "That *can't* happen."

"Then, we should try it!" RoRo said eagerly.

So, we did. We closed our eyes and slowly counted to five. *"One...two...three...four...five."*

All of a sudden, we disappeared!

When we opened our eyes, it was dark...
and we noticed something *very strange*!
We were floating...in space!

"RoRo, this is *so* cool!" I shouted. "I think we should go exploring. Let's check out the moon! I sure hope it's made of cheese since we haven't had lunch yet."

It took us two hours to float to the moon. When we got there, part of it *was* made of cheese. So, we took a few bites, and it was delicious!

"This is great!" said Jack, picking up a moon rock. "We have always dreamed of going into space. Instead of seeing it through our telescopes, we are seeing everything up close. I'm going to take this moon rock home, so our friends will believe us when we tell them about our adventure."

"Let's have some more fun before we go home," Camille said. How often do you get to go to space? I think we should choose something that we have always wanted to do in space, and then we can go home."

"Since we are done eating, we should find a comfortable crater to sit in and count the stars," Tippy said.

"I don't know if that's a good idea Tippy," Ooboo replied. "Look at what counting got us into."

The friends agreed, so they all sat in a crater and started counting stars.

"One...two...three..."

Then, RoRo and Camille wanted each of them to point to a group of stars and name a constellation after themselves.

"How about naming mine *Tippy Over,* because it's over there?" Tippy asked. The friends started giggling.

Jack's idea was next. "Let's write our names on the moon so we can see them with our telescopes when we get home."

They all sat down and began writing.

It was getting late, and Ooboo was becoming worried. "I think we should think about going home," he said.

RoRo had a worried look on his face. "Uh, Ooboo. I wanted to tell you this earlier, but we were having so much fun. The magical rocket I bought was a one-way rocketship. We *can't* get home."

"There *must* be a way to get home," said Ooboo.

As he was staring into space, a shooting star went zooming by. At that moment, he wished for a way to get home.

All of a sudden, a phone booth appeared.

Ooboo and his friends floated over to the phone booth, where he quickly picked up the phone and called 9-1-1.

After a few rings, a lady answered. "9-1-1, what's your emergency?" she asked.

"Hello. My name is Ooboo, and my friends and I are stuck in space."

"Well, now. How did that happen?" she asked.

"My friend RoRo gave me a magical, one-way rocketship for my birthday," I answered.

"Don't worry, Ooboo," she said. "By the way, is the moon made of cheese?"

"Part of it is!" I responded. "Cool, huh? So, how do we get home?"

"Oh, no problem," the operator said. "Do you see the letters located on the dial pad?"

"Yes," I said.

"Do you know how to spell Earth?" she asked.

"Of course," I answered. "I am Ooboo, the smartest kangaroo alive!"

"Ok," she said. "Press the letters to spell Earth. After you are done, you and your friends should close your eyes and slowly count to five. When you are done, you should be home."

I did exactly what the operator told me to do.
I spelled Earth on the dial pad, we closed our
eyes, and then slowly counted to five.

One...two...three...four...five.

In an instant, we were home! We were so happy!

"We made it!" we said together.

"I knew we would," RoRo said with a smile.

"Let's go open the rest of the presents," I said.

Tippy gave me a jump rope and Camille gave me a soccer ball.

Finally, I opened my gift from Jack. It was a miniature airplane. We all knew where this was going, but I still had to be sure...

"Jack, is this a magical plane?" I asked puzzled.

"Yes," said Jack, throwing his hands in the air with excitement, "and it can take us on unlimited rides!"

Ooboo, RoRo, Camille, Jack, and Tippy smiled.
"Where should we go next?" they all said at once.

And before we knew it, our adventures were just
beginning...

50888223R00024

Made in the USA
San Bernardino, CA
07 July 2017